2060

by Bruce Goldwell

Copyright © 2024 Bruce Goldwell

All rights reserved

Disclaimer: This work of fiction contains characters, events, and situations that are entirely products of the author's imagination *or are they*? Any resemblance to actual persons [except Donald J. Trump], living or dead, or real events is purely coincidental. The author has created a fictional world for storytelling purposes, and any similarities to individuals or events in the real world are unintentional. The opinions, actions, and characteristics of the characters in this narrative are fictional and do not represent the views or beliefs of any real persons. Reader discretion is advised, and the content is intended for entertainment purposes only.

Table of Contents

2060 7
- Introduction..9
- A New Era Begins (2025)..........................17
  - The Election of 2025 and the End of Conflict...17
  - The Largest Deportation in History..........21
  - A Historic Peace Accord: Israel and Palestine 26
  - NESARA Takes the Stage 30
  - The Dawn of Medbed Technology 35
- Technological and Economic Renaissance 40
  - The Global Health Revolution 40
  - Financial Systems Re-imagined.................45
  - A New Age of Agriculture.........................55
- Societal Transformation (2035) 64
  - Eradicating Poverty and Homelessness 64
  - Enhancing Quality of Life..........................69
  - A Renaissance of Leisure and Creativity...75
  - Evolution of Global Governance 80
  - Fostering International Peace and Cooperation 81
- Sustaining Utopia (2040-50's) 85
  - Navigating a Doubling Population..............85
  - Upholding the Utopian Vision 89
  - The Vanguard of Technological Innovation94
- Reflections on a World Transformed...............99
  - The Catalyst of Change: Donald Trump's Presidency 99
  - Evaluating NESARA and GESARA's

- Global Impact 104
- Envisioning the Future Beyond 2060 110
- Conclusion 115
- Summarizing the Journey to Utopia 115
- Lessons for a Sustainable Future 120
- NESARA and GESARA Unveiled 125
- The Revolution of Medbed Technology .. 131
- Epilogue 135
- Bruce Goldwell's 140
- Web Site 140
- QFS, Nesara/Gesara, and 2060 143
- About The Author 146

2060

"Wisdom isn't knowing everything-
it's knowing when to learn from others."

Introduction

In the year 2024, the world stood at a pivotal crossroads. Global tensions simmered across continents, with geopolitical conflicts, economic instability, and social disparities casting long shadows over the future of humanity. The specter of climate change loomed larger than ever, threatening irreversible damage to our planet's delicate ecosystems. Societies grappled with the dual challenges of advancing technology and widening inequality, raising profound questions about the direction of human progress.

Amidst this backdrop of uncertainty, a sense of urgency for transformative change pervaded the collective consciousness. The world yearned for solutions that could bridge divides, heal the planet, and usher in an era of lasting peace and prosperity. It was within this crucible of challenges that the stage was set for a series of events that would fundamentally alter the course of history.

As 2024 unfolded, the international community faced these trials with a mixture of apprehension and hope. The ongoing conflicts in regions like Eukrania and the persistent threat of war cast a pall over global affairs. Economic systems, burdened by debt and inequality, seemed increasingly untenable, prompting calls for radical reform. Meanwhile, the relentless march of technology offered both promise and peril, as societies struggled to reconcile the benefits of innovation with the imperative of ensuring equitable access and ethical governance.

Yet, it was precisely at this juncture of crisis and opportunity that a vision for a new future began to coalesce. A future where the swords of war could be beaten into plowshares, where the chains of debt and poverty were broken, and where the bounty of technological advancement was shared by all. This vision was galvanized by the prospect of groundbreaking political and economic reforms, epitomized by the impending activation of NESARA (National Economic Security and Reformation Act) in the United States and its global counterpart, GESARA (Global Economic Security and Reformation Act).

The year 2025 would mark the beginning of this transformative journey, catalyzed by the election of Donald Trump as President of the United States. His administration would come to play a pivotal role in not only ending the Eukrania-Russian war but also in championing the principles of NESARA and GESARA, setting the stage for a series of reforms that promised to reshape the world. The global adoption of these acts heralded the dawn of a new era, one characterized by financial freedom, technological marvels like Medbeds, and a renewed commitment to human welfare and environmental stewardship.

As this book unfolds, it will chronicle the historical account of how, from the tumultuous times of 2024, the world embarked on a path toward a utopian future. Through the lens of this narrative, we will explore the milestones and innovations that paved the way to 2060, a year when humanity, having embraced the principles of peace, prosperity, and sustainability, flourished like never before. This is the story of how the world changed, guided by visionary leadership and the indomitable spirit of cooperation among nations, to ensure a legacy of progress for generations to come.

The book's core narrative:

The transformative era from 2024 to 2060, sparked by significant political and technological changes. At the heart of this narrative lies the transformative era spanning from 2024 to 2060, a period marked by profound political and technological changes that redefined the contours of human society. This era witnessed the dismantling of longstanding barriers to peace and prosperity, driven by visionary leadership and groundbreaking innovations that catalyzed a global renaissance.

The journey commenced with a pivotal moment in 2025, when Donald Trump's election to the Presidency of the United States ignited the fuse of transformation. His administration, characterized by bold diplomacy and decisive action, brought an immediate end to the protracted Eukrania-Russian conflict, setting a precedent for global cooperation and conflict resolution. This act of statesmanship not only averted further escalation but also heralded a new chapter in international relations, where dialogue and mutual respect paved the way for enduring peace.

Simultaneously, the introduction and activation of

NESARA in the United States, followed by the global embrace of GESARA, signified a radical departure from traditional economic policies and practices. These reforms, steeped in principles of equity and sustainability, promised a world where financial freedom was not just a privilege for a few but a fundamental right for all. The sweeping changes proposed by these acts—ranging from debt forgiveness to the abolition of income tax and the introduction of new, asset-backed currencies—were aimed at rectifying the imbalances of the past and laying the foundation for a more just and prosperous global economy.

Parallel to these political upheavals, the era was characterized by an explosion of technological innovation that transformed every aspect of daily life. Among the most significant of these advances were Medbeds, a revolutionary healthcare technology capable of eradicating diseases and restoring bodily functions to their optimal state.

The widespread deployment of Medbeds under Trump's presidency marked a quantum leap in medical science, extending human lifespan and significantly enhancing the quality of life across the globe.

Moreover, this period saw remarkable advancements in sustainable energy, agriculture, and transportation, including the realization of flying cars, which had long been the stuff of science fiction. These technologies enabled humanity to meet the challenges of a rapidly growing population, ensuring that the basic needs of every individual were met without compromising the health of our planet.

The narrative of 2024 to 2060 is, therefore, one of unprecedented change, characterized by the dissolution of old paradigms and the emergence of a new world order. It is a story of how humanity, faced with existential threats, chose the path of innovation, compassion, and unity. This book aims to chronicle this remarkable journey, exploring the milestones that defined this era and the ways in which they reshaped the world. Through this exploration, we seek to understand not just the events that occurred but the lessons they impart for future generations, as we continue to strive for a world where every individual has the opportunity to live a life of dignity, fulfillment, and joy.

A New Era Begins (2025)

The Election of 2025 and the End of Conflict

The year 2025 emerged as a watershed moment in the annals of history, heralding a new chapter of peace and prosperity with the election of Donald Trump as President of the United States. In a world teetering on the brink of escalating conflicts and deepening geopolitical divisions, the outcome of the U.S. presidential election was watched with bated breath. Trump's victory was not just a political turnover; it was the prelude to a series of actions that would dramatically alter the course of global events.

Immediately following his inauguration, President Trump embarked on an ambitious diplomatic mission to bring an end to the protracted Eukrania-Russian war. This conflict, which had simmered and occasionally boiled over into open warfare, stood as a symbol of the old world order, characterized by mistrust, rivalry, and relentless competition for dominance. Trump, leveraging his background in deal-making and negotiations, opened direct and unprecedented channels of communication with both Ukrainian and Russian leaders.

The negotiations were intense and fraught with decades of historical grievances, but Trump's unorthodox approach gradually began to break down the barriers. His strategy focused on mutual benefits and the shared prosperity that peace would bring, not just to the warring nations but to the global community. After months of painstaking diplomacy, an agreement was reached. The peace deal, brokered with the direct involvement of President Trump, was hailed as a triumph of diplomacy over division. It promised not only to end the hostilities but also to lay the groundwork for a new era of cooperation and stability in the region.

The immediate effects of the peace agreement were palpable. Global markets, long jittery over the prospects of an escalation, responded with optimism, and a collective sigh of relief was felt around the world. The cessation of the Eukrania-Russian war served as a powerful testament to what could be achieved when nations chose dialogue over conflict, a theme that would come to define the era.

This remarkable achievement set the stage for the transformative changes that were to follow. It demonstrated Trump's commitment to his vision of a world where traditional foes could become partners in building a future marked by peace and mutual prosperity. The end of the Eukrania-Russian conflict was not just an end to fighting; it was the beginning of a broader global realignment, where old animosities were set aside in pursuit of a shared vision for humanity.

As the world looked on, the success of these negotiations inspired a sense of possibility. If one of the most intractable conflicts of the early 21st century could be resolved, what other age-old disputes could be brought to an end? The election of 2025 and the subsequent peace deal became a beacon of hope, signaling the dawn of a new era— an era where diplomacy triumphed, and the stage was set for the sweeping reforms and innovations that would define the coming decades.

The Largest Deportation in History

One of the most pressing issues facing the United States in recent years has been the need to address and stabilize border issues, particularly concerning immigration. Under the administration of President Donald Trump, significant efforts were made to tackle this issue head-on, resulting in the initiation of the largest deportation campaign targeting individuals who crossed the border between Mexico and the USA without proper authorization. While controversial, this aggressive stance on immigration had unexpected consequences, ultimately proving beneficial for both the deported individuals and the countries to which they were returned.

The Trump administration's stance on immigration was characterized by a hardline approach aimed at securing the nation's borders and enforcing existing immigration laws. Central to this approach was the implementation of policies designed to deter illegal border crossings and streamline the deportation process for individuals found to be residing in the country unlawfully. As a result, thousands of undocumented immigrants, primarily from Central and South America, were deported to their countries of origin.

While the deportation measures sparked intense debate and criticism, particularly from human rights advocates and immigrant rights groups, there emerged an unforeseen outcome that would have far-reaching implications. Many of those deported found themselves returning to countries that were undergoing transformative changes, thanks to the activation of NESARA (National Economic Security and Recovery Act) and GESARA (Global Economic Security and Recovery Act) principles.

NESARA and GESARA, long the subject of

speculation and debate, were purported to be comprehensive economic reform initiatives aimed at promoting prosperity and well-being for citizens worldwide. Under the principles of NESARA and GESARA, countries around the globe experienced positive shifts in their economies and societies, leading to improved living standards and increased opportunities for their citizens.

As a result of the activation of NESARA and GESARA principles, citizens in all countries began to reap the benefits of these positive changes. Economic stability, job growth, and improved access to essential services became the norm, transforming communities and empowering individuals to thrive in their own countries. With newfound opportunities for prosperity and advancement, the need for migration as a means of seeking a better life in another country diminished significantly.

For those who had been deported from the United States, the activation of NESARA and GESARA proved to be a silver lining amidst their hardship. Returning to their home countries, they found themselves entering societies that were undergoing rapid transformation and experiencing newfound prosperity. Jobs were more plentiful, education and healthcare were more accessible, and opportunities for economic and social advancement abounded.

The activation of NESARA and GESARA principles had a ripple effect that extended far beyond the borders of any one country. As nations around the world embraced these principles and implemented reforms to align with their objectives, a global wave of positive change swept across continents, lifting millions out of poverty and paving the way for a brighter future for all.

In conclusion, while the issue of immigration and border security remains complex and multifaceted, the initiation of NESARA and GESARA principles has provided a pathway to addressing the underlying causes driving migration. By fostering economic prosperity and stability on a global scale, NESARA and GESARA have enabled citizens in all countries to prosper in their own homelands, ultimately reducing the need for migration as a means of seeking a better life elsewhere.

A Historic Peace Accord: Israel and Palestine

In the wake of resolving the Eukrania-Russian conflict, President Trump turned his attention to one of the longest-standing and most complex geopolitical issues of our time: the Israeli-Palestinian conflict. Building on the momentum of his diplomatic success, Trump embarked on what many considered an impossible mission—achieving a lasting peace between Israel and Palestine. Through a series of high-stakes negotiations, marked by an unprecedented level of engagement from all parties involved, a historic peace accord was reached.

This peace agreement was unlike any before. It recognized the mutual rights of Israelis and Palestinians to self-determination, security, and prosperity. But what truly set it apart was its broader vision: the accord did not merely seek to end hostilities but aimed to foster a deep, lasting respect among all religions and cultures in the region. Trump's administration facilitated dialogues that encouraged empathy, understanding, and respect for the "other," transcending the traditional political solutions to touch the hearts and minds of people on both sides.

A core component of this peace accord was the commitment from governments worldwide to abstain from financing or supporting wars for a duration of 1,000 years. This bold declaration, known as the Millennium Pact, aimed to solidify a global consensus against the use of war as a means to resolve disputes. The hope was that, with a millennium of peace, future generations would come to find the very notion of war abhorrent and obsolete.

This agreement sparked a global movement towards tolerance and mutual respect. Religious leaders across the spectrum—Jews, Muslims, Christians, and others—came forward to support this new paradigm, engaging in dialogues that emphasized common values over differences. The idea that all individuals had the right to believe according to the dictates of their own conscience became a foundational principle of this new era.

The impact of this peace accord was profound and far-reaching. It served as a catalyst for peace worldwide, inspiring similar agreements in other conflict zones and encouraging a global reassessment of how societies approach religious and cultural differences. The vision of a world where every religion and culture could coexist in harmony began to take shape, influencing policies, education, and social norms across the globe.

The Israeli-Palestinian peace accord, under Trump's leadership, thus became more than just a resolution to a longstanding conflict. It was a beacon of hope and a testament to the power of understanding and respect in overcoming generations of discord and division. This monumental achievement not only reshaped the Middle Eastern landscape but also set a precedent for the entire world, marking the beginning of a new chapter in human history—a chapter where peace, tolerance, and mutual respect form the pillars of global society.

NESARA Takes the Stage

In the euphoria following the unprecedented diplomatic successes of 2025, President Trump and his administration embarked on an equally ambitious domestic agenda. Central to this was the initiation of the National Economic Security and Reformation Act (NESARA), a legislative proposal that promised to redefine the American financial system and, by extension, set a precedent for economic reform worldwide.

NESARA was born from a vision of economic justice and equity. It sought to address the systemic flaws within the U.S. financial system—flaws that had perpetuated inequality, burdened citizens with unsustainable debt, and undermined the stability of the economy. The act proposed sweeping reforms aimed at rectifying these issues, including the forgiveness of mortgage and student loan debt, the abolition of income tax, and the re-establishment of a gold-backed currency. These measures were designed not only to reset the financial landscape but also to liberate the average citizen from the cycles of debt and dependency that had constrained economic growth and innovation.

The announcement of NESARA was met with a mixture of astonishment and skepticism. Proponents hailed it as a revolutionary step towards a fairer and more prosperous society, while critics dismissed it as utopian and unfeasible. Nonetheless, the Trump administration pressed forward, leveraging the momentum of their diplomatic victories to galvanize support for the act.

As NESARA began to take effect, its impact was immediate and profound. Debt forgiveness initiatives released millions of Americans from the shackles of financial burden, sparking a surge in consumer confidence and economic activity. The abolition of income tax, once a contentious proposition, was celebrated as a triumph of fiscal policy, significantly enhancing the disposable income of ordinary citizens. Meanwhile, the transition to a gold-backed currency restored faith in the American dollar, stabilizing the economy and reasserting the United States' position in the global financial order.

The global response to NESARA was equally significant. Inspired by the U.S.'s bold initiative, countries around the world began to consider similar reforms under the umbrella of GESARA—the Global Economic Security and Reformation Act. This international movement towards economic reform represented a collective aspiration for a new economic paradigm—one characterized by stability, equity, and sustainability.

However, the path to implementing NESARA was not without its challenges. The act required a fundamental restructuring of the banking and financial systems, a process that encountered resistance from entrenched interests and institutions wary of change. Moreover, the global coordination required to align GESARA with diverse economic policies and conditions presented a complex diplomatic puzzle.

Despite these obstacles, the spirit of innovation and the pursuit of a common good drove the initiative forward. The implementation of NESARA became a testament to the possibility of transformative change, setting a new standard for economic policy and inspiring a global reevaluation of the principles underlying financial systems.

As the world watched, the United States embarked on a bold experiment to redefine prosperity and economic freedom. NESARA's implementation marked a pivotal moment in the journey towards a more equitable and prosperous future, laying the groundwork for the global shifts that would follow in the years to come.

The Dawn of Medbed Technology

Amid the sweeping economic reforms and diplomatic victories of the late 2020s, another groundbreaking development was set to revolutionize the world: the introduction of Medbed technology. Under the auspices of President Trump's administration, this advanced technology, long the subject of speculation and anticipation, was unveiled to the public, promising a new era in healthcare and human wellness.

Medbed technology, derived from years of clandestine research and development, possessed the ability to diagnose, treat, and heal a wide array of diseases and injuries with unparalleled precision and effectiveness. Utilizing principles of quantum healing and regenerative medicine, Medbeds could restore damaged tissues, eradicate diseases at the cellular level, and even reverse the aging process, offering the promise of prolonged life and near-perfect health.

The deployment of Medbed technology came at a critical juncture. The world's healthcare systems were buckling under the strain of aging populations, chronic diseases, and the escalating costs of medical care. Medbeds offered a solution that was not only innovative but also equitable. President Trump envisioned a world where access to this life-saving technology was not a privilege of the wealthy but a fundamental right available to all, a vision that resonated deeply with the global populace.

The impact of Medbed technology on society was profound. Hospitals and clinics were equipped with these devices, making once-incurable diseases a thing of the past and transforming the landscape of healthcare delivery. The psychological and social implications were equally significant; individuals who had resigned themselves to a life defined by illness or disability found new hope and vitality. The promise of extended life expectancy and enhanced quality of life ignited discussions about the social, economic, and ethical implications of such a shift.

The global roll-out of Medbed technology, facilitated by cooperative international agreements and the support of the GESARA framework, ensured that these benefits were not confined to any single nation. Countries around the world joined in the effort to make Medbeds accessible to their citizens, catalyzing a worldwide health renaissance. This global initiative was underpinned by the principle that the well-being of each individual was integral to the prosperity and harmony of the global community.

However, the introduction of Medbed technology was not without its challenges. The medical establishment, pharmaceutical companies, and the broader healthcare industry faced unprecedented disruption. Traditional healthcare models had to be reevaluated and restructured to accommodate the capabilities of Medbed technology. Ethical debates emerged over the implications of such profound medical advancements, particularly regarding longevity and population growth.

Despite these hurdles, the promise of Medbed technology inspired a collective endeavor to overcome them. The Trump administration, in partnership with international leaders and organizations, worked tirelessly to address these challenges, ensuring that the benefits of Medbeds were realized in a responsible and equitable manner.

The dawn of Medbed technology marked a pivotal moment in human history. As the 2030s approached, the world stood on the brink of a new age—an age of unparalleled health and vitality.

This era of medical marvels was not merely about curing disease; it was about re-imagining the potential of human life. The legacy of Medbed technology, with its promise of healing and rejuvenation, would resonate through the decades, fundamentally altering the course of human evolution and setting the stage for the remarkable transformations that were yet to come.

Technological and Economic Renaissance

The Global Health Revolution

The decade of 2025-2035 will be remembered as the era when humanity triumphed over disease and began to redefine the limits of human lifespan, thanks to the global dissemination of Medbed technology. This groundbreaking advancement in healthcare, initially met with skepticism, soon proved to be the cornerstone of a worldwide health revolution, fundamentally transforming how medical care was administered and experienced across the globe.

The Journey of Global Distribution

The roll-out of Medbed technology on a global scale was an endeavor marked by unprecedented cooperation among nations. Faced with logistical, regulatory, and economic hurdles, countries came together under the banner of shared humanity to ensure that this life-altering technology reached every corner of the planet. International agreements facilitated the distribution of Medbeds, prioritizing accessibility in underdeveloped regions where traditional healthcare infrastructure was sparse or non-existent. This collaborative effort was buoyed by NGOs and private sector partnerships, pooling resources to overcome the financial and logistical challenges of deployment.

Eradicating Diseases and Extending Life

The impact of widespread access to Medbed technology was profound and immediate. Diseases that had plagued humanity for centuries, from cancers to chronic illnesses, were now treatable with an efficiency and effectiveness previously unimaginable. The technology's ability to repair cellular damage and restore bodily functions meant that not only were diseases cured, but the aging process itself was slowed, allowing for longer, healthier lives.

This section delves into the personal stories of those whose lives were transformed by Medbed technology. From a young child in a remote village healed from a congenital heart defect to an elderly woman in a metropolitan city who regained her vitality, these narratives underscore the deep, personal impact of the global health revolution.

Societal and Ethical Implications

With the advent of Medbed technology, societies worldwide faced the task of adapting to new norms of health and longevity. The prospect of extended lifespans prompted a reevaluation of societal structures, from employment and retirement to social welfare and intergenerational relationships.

This section explores the ethical considerations that arose, including questions of resource allocation, population growth, and the potential for socioeconomic disparities in access to Medbed treatments.

As the world navigated these challenges, the ethos of the health revolution evolved. It became clear that Medbed technology was not just a tool for curing diseases but a catalyst for re-imagining the potential of human life. Governments, healthcare providers, and communities worked to address the ethical dilemmas, ensuring that the benefits of Medbeds were realized equitably and responsibly.

The global health revolution of the 2030s, fueled by the widespread adoption of Medbed technology, marked a pivotal moment in human history. It was an era defined by unprecedented advancements in healthcare, the eradication of diseases, and the extension of human life. As the world looked towards the future, it did so with the knowledge that the possibilities for health and longevity were now broader and more attainable than ever before. The legacy of this revolution would be felt in the decades to come, shaping the course of human evolution and setting new horizons for what humanity could achieve.

Financial Systems Re-imagined

The 2030s were not only a period of medical marvels but also a time of profound economic transformation. The global implementation of NESARA and GESARA reshaped the financial landscape, ushering in a new era of economic equity and stability. This segment explores the sweeping changes these acts introduced and the impact they had on both the macroeconomic environment and the lives of individuals worldwide.

The Foundation of NESARA and GESARA

At the heart of this economic revolution were NESARA in the United States and its global counterpart, GESARA. Envisioned as comprehensive reforms to rectify the systemic imbalances of the past, these acts aimed to liberate the world from the clutches of debt, unfair taxation, and opaque financial systems. Debt forgiveness, the abolition of income taxes, and the introduction of asset-backed currencies were among the bold measures adopted to achieve these goals.

The rationale behind the implementation of these reforms, envisioning a future where economic systems prioritize the well-being of every individual in society rather than catering to a privileged few. It delves into the initial challenges faced when undertaking such ambitious transformations, including navigating legal disputes and overhauling complex international banking and financial structures.

The core intent behind these changes, underscores the transition towards fostering an economy that is fair and all-encompassing. The changes are designed with the aim of uplifting every individual, irrespective of their financial standing, propelling a sense of unity and mutual benefit.

As the new initiatives took root, they encountered friction against established statutes and economic systems that need to be revised to reflect this new equitable vision. It throws light on the complexities in modifying global banking and monetary systems, which necessitates international cooperation to guarantee a seamless evolution.

Despite these initial setbacks, the text infers that the advantages to be gained from these adjustments are significant. By re-calibrating economic processes with a focus on societal welfare, there's an opportunity to diminish poverty, bridge wealth disparities, and drive consistent economic advancement worldwide.

In essence, an inspiring vision unfolded of a future molded by financial structures aimed at benefiting the broader population rather than a select few.

Although there may be hurdles along this path, the end goal of realizing a fair and impartial society fuels persistent dedication to champion and maintain these pivotal changes.

The Ripple Effects of Economic Reform

The effects of NESARA and GESARA were both immediate and far-reaching. Debt forgiveness initiatives wiped clean the slates of millions, freeing them from the burden of mortgages, student loans, and other financial obligations. The abolition of income tax put more money into the pockets of the populace, stimulating economic activity and increasing the overall standard of living.

A comprehensive analysis reveals that the introduction of new, stable currencies backed by tangible assets such as gold and silver has restored confidence in the global financial markets. It underscores the shift from a debt-based economy to one anchored in actual value and explores the resultant effects on trade, investment, and international relations.

Navigating the New Economic Landscape

The global adoption of GESARA principles marked a pivotal shift in the way nations approached economic policy and governance. This section explores the collaborative efforts required to align national policies with the overarching goals of GESARA, highlighting the diplomatic negotiations and international cooperation that paved the way for a more equitable global economy.

Personal stories and case studies illustrate the tangible impacts of these economic reforms on individuals and communities. From small business owners who flourished in the new economic environment to families who experienced financial freedom for the first time, these narratives bring to life the human aspect of the financial revolution.

1. Maria's Journey to Entrepreneurial Success:
Maria, a single mother living in a rural village, had always dreamed of starting her own business but faced numerous barriers due to financial constraints and limited access to resources. However, with the implementation of economic reforms prioritizing small business development and microfinance initiatives, Maria saw an opportunity to turn her dream into reality. Armed with a newfound sense of optimism and support from local community programs, Maria launched her own small bakery. As demand for her delicious pastries grew, so did Maria's confidence and income. Today, Maria's bakery is a thriving enterprise, providing employment opportunities for other members of her community and serving as a testament to the transformative power of economic

empowerment.

2. The Rodriguez Family's Journey to Financial Freedom:

For years, the Rodriguez family struggled to make ends meet, living from paycheck to paycheck and facing constant financial insecurity. However, with the advent of economic reforms aimed at promoting financial literacy and empowering low-income families, the Rodriguezes found a path to stability and prosperity. Through educational programs and access to affordable banking services, they learned to budget effectively, save for the future, and invest wisely. Over time, their diligence and newfound financial knowledge paid off, leading to increased savings, improved credit scores, and ultimately, homeownership. Today, the Rodriguez family enjoys a newfound sense of security and freedom, no longer bound by the constraints of poverty, thanks to the transformative impact of economic reforms on their lives.

3. Carlos's Journey from Unemployment to Economic Empowerment:

After losing his job during a downturn in the economy, Carlos struggled to find steady employment and provide for his family. However, with the implementation of economic reforms prioritizing job creation and workforce development, Carlos found renewed hope and opportunity. Through government-sponsored training programs and incentives for businesses to hire unemployed workers, Carlos gained new skills and secured a job in a growing industry. As he worked his way up the ranks, Carlos not only regained financial stability but also discovered a newfound sense of purpose and fulfillment in his career. Today, Carlos serves as a mentor and advocate for others facing similar challenges, inspiring them to persevere and seize the opportunities made possible by economic reforms.

These personal stories serve as powerful examples of the transformative impact of economic reforms on individuals and communities, showcasing how initiatives aimed at promoting economic empowerment and inclusion can change lives for the better.

Looking Ahead

As the world navigated this re-imagined financial system, questions about sustainability, fairness, and the future of economic governance remained. This section reflects on the lessons learned during the transformative decade of the 2030s and considers the challenges and opportunities that lie ahead.

The legacy of NESARA and GESARA, with their promise of a more just and stable economic foundation, continued to influence global financial policies and practices. As humanity moved forward, the principles embedded in these acts served as a guiding light for future generations, aspiring to a world where economic freedom and prosperity are accessible to all.

Through the lens of this economic renaissance, the 2030s emerged as a decade of hope, challenge, and unprecedented opportunity. The global implementation of NESARA and GESARA not only redefined the essence of economic justice but also set the stage for a future where financial systems are inherently aligned with the principles of equity and sustainability.

A New Age of Agriculture

The transformation of the 2030s extended beyond healthcare and financial systems, revolutionizing the very way humanity sourced its sustenance. This era marked the advent of a new age of agriculture, characterized by technological breakthroughs that not only secured global food security but also redefined the relationship between humanity and the environment.

Innovations in Agricultural Technology

The era was distinguished by rapid advancements in agricultural technology, which promised to meet the needs of a world population that had more than doubled. Precision farming, powered by AI and robotics, optimized the use of resources, ensuring that crops received exactly what they needed for optimal growth, thus significantly reducing waste and increasing yields.

Genetically modified crops, engineered for enhanced yield, nutritional value, and resilience to changing climate conditions, became staples in fields around the globe. Vertical farming, a practice that utilized skyscraper-like structures for crop production, revolutionized urban agriculture, bringing food production closer to urban consumers and drastically reducing the carbon footprint associated with traditional farming and transportation.

Ensuring Global Food Security

These technological innovations played a pivotal role in addressing the challenges posed by the population boom and the pressing need for sustainable food production methods. The chapter explores how these advances ensured a steady, reliable supply of nutritious food, making hunger and malnutrition increasingly rare phenomena.

Case studies from diverse regions provide a vivid picture of how these technologies were adapted and implemented across different climates and agricultural contexts. From the rice paddies of Asia transformed by precision irrigation techniques to urban rooftops in North America blossoming with vertical farms, these stories illustrate the global scale and local impact of the agricultural revolution.

The Socioeconomic Impact

The revolution in food production had profound socioeconomic implications. This section delves into the empowerment of smallholder farmers, who, with access to advanced technologies and practices, could compete on a level playing field with larger agricultural enterprises. It also examines the creation of new job opportunities in the tech-driven agricultural sector and the positive effects on rural economies.

Global trade patterns have shifted due to a rise in food self-sufficiency among countries that previously depended heavily on imports. This shift has not only bolstered local economies but also fostered a more stable and fair worldwide food distribution system.

Environmental and Ethical Considerations

As humanity entered an era of unprecedented technological advancement in agriculture, it also confronted new ethical and environmental challenges. The rapid pace of innovation prompted a critical re-evaluation of practices in food production, sparking debates on topics ranging from genetic modification to concerns about biodiversity.

Navigating Ethical Complexities:

One of the central themes of this era was the ethical implications of agricultural technologies, particularly in the realm of genetic modification. As scientists unlocked the potential to manipulate the genetic makeup of crops to enhance traits such as yield and resistance to pests, questions arose about the unintended consequences and ethical boundaries of such interventions. Debates ensued, with stakeholders weighing the potential benefits against concerns about genetic diversity, food safety, and long-term ecological impacts.

Development of Regulatory Frameworks:

Amidst these debates, regulatory agencies and policymakers worked diligently to establish frameworks that would guide the responsible development and deployment of agricultural technologies. These frameworks aimed to strike a delicate balance, fostering innovation while ensuring that ethical considerations and environmental protection remained paramount. Through rigorous testing, oversight, and public engagement, regulatory bodies sought to mitigate risks and safeguard the interests of consumers, farmers, and the environment alike.

Positive Environmental Impact:

Despite the ethical complexities, the adoption of innovative agricultural technologies yielded significant environmental benefits. By reducing reliance on chemical pesticides and fertilizers, these technologies contributed to lower chemical use and minimized environmental contamination. Additionally, advancements in precision agriculture techniques led to more efficient water use and reduced soil erosion, mitigating the environmental footprint of agricultural production. The narrative celebrates this alignment of human progress with ecological preservation as a hallmark of the era, showcasing how technological innovation can be harnessed to heal the planet while meeting the needs of a growing population.

Embracing Sustainability:

Central to this narrative is the overarching commitment to sustainability, which guided decision-making at every level of agricultural production. From farm-level practices to global policy initiatives, sustainability principles were integrated into strategies for managing natural resources, conserving biodiversity, and mitigating climate change. By prioritizing long-term environmental health and ethical integrity, stakeholders forged a path towards a more resilient and equitable food system, ensuring that future generations would inherit a planet capable of sustaining life in all its diversity.

The era of agricultural innovation was marked by a profound reckoning with ethical and environmental considerations. Through careful regulation, technological innovation, and a steadfast commitment to sustainability, stakeholders navigated complex challenges to create a food system that not only nourished humanity but also nurtured the planet. As we reflect on this transformative period, we are reminded of the enduring importance of ethical stewardship and environmental responsibility in shaping a more prosperous and harmonious future for all.

Looking Forward

The foundations laid by this new age of agriculture promised not only to sustain the burgeoning global population but also to propel humanity towards a future where environmental sustainability and food security went hand in hand. The legacy of this transformative decade was a testament to human ingenuity and its capacity to harmonize the needs of a growing population with the imperatives of planetary health.

This encapsulates a period of unparalleled innovation in agriculture, setting the stage for a future where food is plentiful, nutritious, and produced in harmony with the Earth. It reflects a pivotal shift towards a more sustainable, equitable, and prosperous world for all.

Societal Transformation (2035)

Eradicating Poverty and Homelessness

This period stands as a testament to humanity's capacity for compassion and innovation, marked by the near-eradication of poverty and homelessness across the globe. The decade witnessed the culmination of concerted efforts by governments, non-governmental organizations, and communities, driven by the economic and technological advancements of the previous decades. The strategies implemented were diverse, yet they shared a common goal: to uplift every individual and provide the foundations for a life of dignity and opportunity.

Universal Basic Income: A Foundation for Economic Security

One of the cornerstone policies in this

transformative era was the widespread adoption of Universal Basic Income (UBI) programs. Designed to provide all citizens with a regular, unconditional sum of money, UBI was instrumental in ensuring that basic needs were met, regardless of employment status. This chapter explores the implementation of UBI across various countries, analyzing its impact on reducing poverty levels and stimulating economic activity. Personal stories highlight how UBI served as a lifeline for many, enabling individuals to pursue education, start new businesses, or simply afford the essentials of life.

Affordable Housing Initiatives: Building Communities

Parallel to the introduction of UBI, significant investments were made in affordable housing projects. Governments and private sector partnerships embarked on innovative housing initiatives, utilizing sustainable building technologies to create affordable, eco-friendly homes. This section delves into the policies and technologies that made these projects possible, such as prefabricated construction methods and green building standards. Case studies from cities around the world illustrate the transformative power of secure and affordable housing in rebuilding communities and revitalizing urban areas.

Comprehensive Social Welfare Programs: A Safety Net for All

The eradication of poverty and homelessness also relied heavily on the expansion of comprehensive social welfare programs. These programs addressed the multifaceted nature of poverty, offering support that ranged from healthcare and education to job training and child care services. This segment examines how these programs were tailored to meet the specific needs of diverse populations, effectively creating a safety net that left no one behind. The narratives of individuals who benefited from these programs underscore their critical role in fostering social mobility and equity.

The Impact on Society

The collective impact of UBI, affordable housing initiatives, and comprehensive social welfare programs was profound. Not only did they dramatically reduce poverty and homelessness, but they also sparked a shift in societal attitudes towards social responsibility and collective wellbeing. This section reflects on the broader social implications of these changes, including increased social cohesion, reduced crime rates, and enhanced public health outcomes.

The journey towards eradicating poverty and homelessness in the 2030s was not without its challenges. However, the successes of this decade demonstrated that with political will, innovative policies, and collaborative efforts, it is possible to address some of humanity's most persistent challenges. As the world moved forward, the lessons learned during this transformative period continued to inspire and guide efforts to create a more equitable and compassionate global society.

Enhancing Quality of Life

The 2030s were characterized not only by remarkable technological advancements and economic reforms but also by profound shifts in societal values and lifestyles. As financial well-being, health, and longevity improved for the majority of the global population, cultures and societies witnessed significant transformations in how life was perceived and lived. This period, marked by an enhanced quality of life, redefined the concept of prosperity, prioritizing personal fulfillment, community engagement, and environmental stewardship alongside economic success.

Redefining Work-Life Balance

With the advent of AI and robotics automating many traditional jobs, and the introduction of Universal Basic Income (UBI), the necessity to work solely for survival diminished. This shift allowed individuals to reconsider their work-life balance, choosing professions not just for financial gain but for personal satisfaction and social contribution. This chapter explores how societies adapted to these new norms, with stories of people transitioning to part-time work, pursuing careers in arts and philanthropy, or dedicating themselves to lifelong learning and community service.

Evolution of Family Dynamics

Improved health and extended lifespans also transformed family structures and dynamics. Multi-generational households became more common, with four or even five generations living under one roof, sharing responsibilities, and enriching each other's lives with their diverse experiences. This section delves into the implications of these changes, from the shifting roles within families to the evolution of support systems and communal living arrangements that emerged as responses to the new societal norms.

Prioritizing Personal Fulfillment

The abundance of resources, including time, and the absence of financial precarity, ushered in an era where personal fulfillment became a societal hallmark. People now had the freedom to explore their passions, develop new skills, and engage in creative and intellectual pursuits without the pressure of financial constraints. This chapter examines the cultural renaissance sparked by this newfound freedom, showcasing the diversity of interests and hobbies that flourished, from art and music to science and exploration.

Community Engagement and Environmental Stewardship

As individual well-being improved, so did the collective consciousness around environmental sustainability and community welfare. This period saw a surge in grassroots movements dedicated to environmental conservation, community building, and social justice. Volunteerism and activism became widespread, with communities coming together to protect natural habitats, support vulnerable populations, and advocate for global peace and cooperation. This highlights the role of community engagement in shaping a more compassionate, sustainable world, featuring stories of impactful initiatives and the individuals behind them.

The Broader Implications

The societal transformations of the 2030s had far-reaching implications, affecting everything from urban planning and education to healthcare and governance. Cities became more livable, with green spaces, community centers, and cultural venues designed to support the well-being of their inhabitants. Education systems evolved to emphasize critical thinking, creativity, and lifelong learning, preparing individuals to thrive in a rapidly changing world. Healthcare became more holistic, focusing on preventative care and mental health alongside medical treatments.

The enhanced quality of life marked a pivotal shift in human history, demonstrating that when societies prioritize the well-being of their citizens, they unlock the potential for a level of prosperity, creativity, and harmony previously unimagined. This era set a new standard for what it means to lead a fulfilling life, offering valuable lessons for future generations on the importance of balancing material success with personal and collective well-being.

A Renaissance of Leisure and Creativity

These advances heralded a new golden age of leisure and creativity, catalyzed by advancements in AI and robotics that significantly reduced the average workweek and liberated individuals to pursue their passions. This era witnessed an unprecedented flourishing of arts and culture, as people around the globe embraced the opportunity to express themselves creatively and explore the diverse tapestries of human expression.

The Liberation of Time

As AI and robotics assumed the brunt of manual and cognitive labor, the concept of work underwent a radical transformation. The reduction of work hours was not merely an economic adjustment but a societal shift that placed a premium on personal time and freedom. This segment delves into how this newfound abundance of leisure time enabled individuals to break free from the traditional 9-to-5 routine, fostering an environment where engagement in cultural, artistic, and intellectual pursuits became the norm rather than the exception.

Flourishing of the Arts

The surge in leisure time led to a renaissance in the arts. Galleries, theaters, and concert halls experienced a revival, with attendance numbers soaring as more people sought out artistic and cultural experiences. This section explores the explosion of creativity across various mediums—painting, sculpture, music, literature, and dance. It highlights the emergence of new artistic movements and the revival of traditional forms, illustrating how the democratization of artistic expression enriched cultural landscapes worldwide.

The Written Word and Beyond

Literature, too, enjoyed a resurgence during this period. The segment examines how digital platforms and self-publishing tools lowered barriers to entry, allowing a diversity of voices to be heard. Book clubs and literary festivals proliferated, fostering a global dialogue around stories and ideas. This section also touches on the expansion of other forms of storytelling, including virtual reality experiences and interactive narratives, which blended traditional storytelling with cutting-edge technology to create immersive experiences.

Cultural Activities and Community Engagement

With an abundance of leisure time at their disposal, community members have turned cultural activities into the bedrock of social life. This shift highlights the vibrancy inherent in community art projects, local theater productions, and music festivals, which serve as focal points for gathering, strengthening social bonds, and celebrating a shared cultural legacy. These activities provide more than just personal growth and creative outlets; they are pivotal in nurturing social unity and fostering an understanding among different factions within communities and between diverse communities themselves.

Impact on Society and Individual Well-being

The renaissance of leisure and creativity had profound implications for society and individual well-being. This section reflects on the psychological and social benefits of engagement in the arts and cultural activities, including improved mental health, increased empathy, and a deeper appreciation for the diversity of human experience. It argues that the cultural flourishing of the 2040s was not merely a byproduct of technological progress but a critical component of a more humane and fulfilled society.

This period paints a vivid image of arts and culture not merely being accessible, but essential to everyday life. It was an era marked by a widespread appreciation for leisure and creativity, which led to a richer and more vibrant society. This reminds us of the incredible capacity of the human spirit for creation and connection.

Evolution of Global Governance

The societal transformations of the 2030s necessitated and inspired a corresponding evolution in global governance. This period saw a significant shift in how nations approached leadership and policy-making, driven by a collective realization that the well-being of citizens and the sustainability of the planet were paramount. Governments worldwide began to recalibrate their priorities, focusing on peace, cooperation, and the holistic health of their populations and the environment.

Prioritizing Citizen Well-being

At the heart of this new governance paradigm was a commitment to the well-being of citizens. Policies were increasingly evaluated not just on their economic merits but on their ability to enhance quality of life. It was a time of innovative social programs, healthcare reforms, and environmental policies that have arisen, demonstrating how governments aimed to build more equitable, healthy, and sustainable societies. It examines the impact of these policies in instilling a feeling of security and belonging in citizens, which contributed to increased happiness and societal cohesion.

Fostering International Peace and Cooperation

The period marked by a renewed emphasis on international peace and cooperation. In an era where the interconnectedness of global challenges was ever more apparent, nations recognized the necessity of working together to address issues such as climate change, resource scarcity, and global health threats. This section examines the formation of new international alliances and the strengthening of existing institutions, highlighting how diplomatic efforts led to significant reductions in armed conflicts and the establishment of collaborative frameworks for addressing global challenges.

Adapting to Technological Advancements

The rapid pace of technological advancement presented both opportunities and challenges for governance. As AI and robotics became integral to economies and societies, governments had to navigate issues related to job displacement, privacy, and ethical use of technology. There were regulatory approaches and ethical guidelines developed to manage these advancements, ensuring they benefited society as a whole. It also looks at how governments leveraged technology to improve public services, enhance transparency, and engage more effectively with citizens.

Engaging Citizens in Governance

An interesting byproduct of the era's advancements was a shift towards more participatory forms of governance. With increased access to information and the proliferation of digital platforms, citizens became more involved in the decision-making processes. This section explores the rise of direct democracy initiatives, citizen assemblies, and other participatory mechanisms that allowed individuals to have a say in shaping the policies and priorities of their governments. It reflects on the impact of this engagement on policy outcomes and public trust in governmental institutions.

Looking Ahead: The Future of Governance

As the 2030s drew to a close, the evolution of global governance had set new standards for leadership, policy-making, and international collaboration. This concluding section contemplates the future trajectory of governance, considering how the lessons learned and the frameworks established during this transformative decade might inform the challenges and opportunities of the future. It posits that the emphasis on well-being, cooperation, and ethical stewardship offers a hopeful blueprint for navigating the complexities of the 21st century and beyond.

The previous information encapsulates a period of profound change in global governance, marked by a shift towards more humane, inclusive, and sustainable approaches to leadership and policy-making. It underscores the indelible link between the well-being of citizens and the health of the planet, heralding a new era of governance that prioritizes the collective good over narrow interests.

Sustaining Utopia (2040-50's)

Navigating a Doubling Population

The decade of the 2050s presented an extraordinary challenge: managing a world where the population had doubled. This period required a re-imagining of how societies could sustainably support an ever-growing number of inhabitants without depleting the planet's resources or compromising the quality of life for future generations.

Innovative Urban Planning

The key to accommodating the burgeoning population lay in innovative urban planning. Cities transformed into models of sustainability and efficiency, incorporating green spaces, renewable energy sources, and smart infrastructure. This section explores the rise of eco-cities, designed to minimize carbon footprints and promote a harmonious balance between urban living and nature. It delves into the integration of vertical gardens, green roofs, and urban farms within city landscapes, illustrating how these features not only contributed to food security but also enhanced the urban aesthetic and air quality.

Resource Management and Ecological Conservation

Effective resource management became paramount as demand surged. Advances in technology facilitated the development of sophisticated water purification and recycling systems, ensuring clean and abundant water for all. Similarly, energy generation shifted towards renewable sources, with solar, wind, and hydroelectric power becoming the backbone of the global energy grid.

Sustainable Living and Community Engagement

Communities embraced zero-waste lifestyles, circular economies, and local sourcing, significantly reducing their environmental impact. The narrative showcases examples of community-led projects that revitalized local ecosystems, from reforestation efforts to the restoration of natural waterways, demonstrating the power of collective action in fostering environmental stewardship.

Adapting to Growth

As the population continued to grow, adaptive technologies and practices were essential in ensuring that expansion could be accommodated without sacrificing sustainability or quality of life. Innovations in construction materials, such as those derived from recycled plastics or engineered to capture carbon, played a critical role in building the infrastructure needed to support the expanded population. Similarly, advancements in transportation technology, including electric and autonomous vehicles, reduced congestion and pollution, making cities more livable and efficient.

Reflections on a Pivotal Decade

This chapter delves into the triumphs and struggles of a world with a population that has doubled. It highlights the critical role of innovation, collaboration, and progressive policies in fostering sustainable, dynamic communities that can meet the needs and ambitions of their people. Examining this significant decade, the narrative showcases the resilience and ingenuity of human societies as they cope with extraordinary expansion, imparting lessons and motivation to future generations tasked with managing the complexities of an increasingly populated and evolving world.

Upholding the Utopian Vision

As the world population surged in the 2050s, the global community faced the critical task of maintaining the utopian vision established by the NESARA and GESARA reforms. This period was characterized by a concerted effort to ensure that the ideals of equity, prosperity, and peace, which had become the hallmarks of the early 21st century, were preserved and extended even as new challenges emerged.

Continual Assessment and Adaptation

The key to sustaining the utopian vision was the recognition that utopia is not a static endpoint but a continuous journey of improvement and adaptation. Governments, international organizations, and civil societies engaged in regular assessments of economic, social, and environmental indicators to identify areas where the vision was falling short.

Addressing Economic Disparities

Despite significant advances, economic disparities remained a stubborn challenge, requiring innovative solutions. This section explores the evolution of economic models to more fully integrate the principles of equity and sustainability. It examines initiatives aimed at further reducing wealth gaps, including progressive taxation systems, universal access to education and healthcare, and investment in sustainable job creation. The narrative also touches on the global effort to ensure that the benefits of technological advancement were equitably shared, preventing the emergence of new forms of economic exclusion.

Strengthening Global Cooperation

The utopian vision of the 2040s was underpinned by unprecedented levels of international cooperation. As the world moved into the 2050s, this spirit of collaboration was tested by the pressures of a growing population and the need for sustainable resource management. There were efforts to strengthen existing alliances and forge new partnerships, focusing on shared goals such as climate action, peacekeeping, and the eradication of poverty. It highlights how these collaborative endeavors were crucial in addressing transnational issues and ensuring a stable, peaceful world.

Emerging Issues and Responsive Governance

The dynamic nature of global society inevitably gave rise to new challenges. From the ethical implications of advanced AI to the management of space exploration and colonization, the 2050s presented scenarios that previous generations had only imagined. This section considers how governments and international bodies responded to these emerging issues, emphasizing the importance of ethical governance, public engagement, and flexible policy frameworks that could adapt to the rapidly changing landscape.

Reflections on a Decade of Stewardship

This reflects on the endeavors of the global community to uphold and advance the utopian vision amidst the complexities of a rapidly evolving world. It showcases the resilience, creativity, and commitment of humanity to build a society that not only meets the needs of its current inhabitants but also secures the well-being of future generations. Through a narrative of continuous effort, collaboration, and innovation, this chapter underscores the enduring aspiration for a world characterized by peace, prosperity, and sustainability.

The Vanguard of Technological Innovation

In the final decade leading to 2060, technological innovation continued to be the linchpin in supporting a burgeoning global population and ensuring the planet's environmental sustainability. This era was marked by groundbreaking advancements that not only addressed immediate challenges but also paved the way for a future where technology and nature coexisted in harmony.

Sustainable Energy Solutions

As the world's energy demands grew with its population, the pursuit of sustainable energy solutions became more critical than ever. The following explores the advancements in solar, wind, and fusion energy technologies that transformed the global energy landscape. It delves into the development of highly efficient solar panels capable of being integrated into all forms of architecture, wind turbines that harnessed the power of the upper atmosphere, and the breakthroughs in fusion energy that promised an almost limitless supply of clean power. These innovations significantly reduced humanity's carbon footprint and underscored the potential of technology to address environmental challenges.

Revolutionizing Food Production

Technological innovation also revolutionized food production, ensuring that a doubled global population could be nourished without further straining the planet's resources. This section examines the advances in vertical farming, hydroponics, and genetically modified organisms (GMOs) designed for higher yields and resilience to changing climate conditions. It highlights how these technologies enabled the efficient production of food in urban environments, reducing the need for transportation and mitigating the impact of agriculture on natural ecosystems.

Water Conservation and Purification

With water scarcity becoming an increasingly pressing issue, technology provided innovative solutions for conservation and purification. The following discusses the development of desalination techniques that made ocean water potable, as well as nanotechnology-based filtration systems that could purify wastewater to drinking water standards. These advancements ensured that clean water was accessible to all, transforming communities that had historically struggled with water scarcity and preventing conflicts over water resources.

Ethical and Sustainable Technological Development

As technological innovations offered solutions to many of the world's challenges, the 2050s also witnessed a growing awareness of the need for ethical and sustainable development. This section reflects on the governance frameworks established to guide the ethical deployment of technology, ensuring that innovations served the common good and did not exacerbate social inequalities or environmental degradation. It considers the role of public discourse and policy-making in shaping the trajectory of technological development, emphasizing the importance of aligning technological advances with the values of equity, sustainability, and respect for nature.

Looking Forward: Technology and the Future of Humanity

We conclude with a forward-looking perspective on the role of technology in shaping the future of humanity. It posits that the innovations of the 2050s, by addressing the immediate needs of a growing population and preserving the planet, have laid the groundwork for a future where technology continues to serve as a force for good. As humanity looks beyond 2060, the lessons learned and the technologies developed during this transformative decade will undoubtedly continue to influence the path towards a sustainable, equitable, and prosperous world for all.

Reflections on a World Transformed

The Catalyst of Change: Donald Trump's Presidency

The period from 2025 to 2060 stands as one of the most transformative eras in human history, a time when the world witnessed unprecedented shifts towards global peace, economic reform, and technological advancement. Central to the initiation of this transformative wave was the presidency of Donald Trump, a tenure that, regardless of political affiliations, undeniably served as a catalyst for significant global changes.

Trump's Diplomatic Achievements

Donald Trump's presidency was marked by a series of bold diplomatic maneuvers that reshaped international relations. His efforts to bring an end to the Eukrania-Russian conflict and facilitate a historic peace agreement between Israel and Palestine not only averted potential escalations but also demonstrated the potential for diplomacy to achieve what many considered impossible. Revisiting these pivotal moments provides an analysis of how Trump's unconventional approach to diplomacy contributed to a rethinking of geopolitical strategies worldwide.

Initiating NESARA and Inspiring GESARA

Beyond his diplomatic achievements, Trump's administration was instrumental in the initiation of the National Economic Security and Reformation Act (NESARA) within the United States, which laid the groundwork for the global adoption of the Global Economic Security and Reformation Act (GESARA). This section delves into the genesis of these acts, examining their objectives, the challenges faced in their implementation, and their profound impact on the global economic landscape. It explores how these reforms aimed to address systemic financial inequalities, promote sustainability, and foster a new era of economic prosperity and stability.

Setting the Stage for Technological and Social Advances

Trump's presidency also coincided with significant technological breakthroughs, notably the introduction and widespread adoption of Medbed technology, which revolutionized healthcare. The following assesses Trump's role in promoting or facilitating these advancements, exploring the interplay between political will, economic policies, and technological innovation. It considers how the administration's policies and initiatives helped set the stage for a period of rapid social and technological progress that would define the subsequent decades.

Reflections on Leadership and Legacy

This chapter reflects on the complex legacy of Donald Trump's presidency, considering both the immediate outcomes and the longer-term implications of his tenure. It discusses how Trump's leadership style, decisions, and policies polarized opinion but undeniably acted as a catalyst for change, pushing the world towards a series of reforms and innovations that might have otherwise taken decades to materialize. Through interviews, expert analysis, and a review of historical data, this section offers a nuanced perspective on the impact of Trump's presidency on the global stage.

Conclusion

In concluding, we do not aim to idolize or vilify Donald Trump but to acknowledge the significant role his presidency played in catalyzing changes that reshaped the world. It presents an objective look at how his tenure influenced the course of global events, setting the groundwork for an era of transformation that would carry on well beyond 2060. This segment invites readers to consider the complex interplay between leadership, policy, and global change, emphasizing the profound impact that political decisions can have on the world's trajectory.

Evaluating NESARA and GESARA's Global Impact

The adoption of the National Economic Security and Reformation Act (NESARA) in the United States, followed by the Global Economic Security and Reformation Act (GESARA), represented a watershed moment in global economic history. Initiated as bold responses to systemic financial inequities, these acts aimed to redefine the essence of economic prosperity and stability on a worldwide scale. This chapter delves into the successes, challenges, and overall impact of NESARA and GESARA from their inception through to 2060, providing a comprehensive evaluation of their role in shaping a new global economic order.

Eradicating Economic Inequalities

One of the most profound impacts of NESARA and GESARA was their contribution to significantly reducing global economic disparities. By implementing mechanisms for debt forgiveness, ensuring more equitable distribution of resources, and restructuring the global banking system, these acts directly addressed the root causes of economic inequality. This section examines the specific policies that were most effective in bridging the wealth gap, supported by statistical analyses and case studies from various countries, illustrating the tangible improvements in the lives of millions.

Fostering Economic Stability and Growth

NESARA and GESARA also played critical roles in stabilizing the global economy and fostering sustainable growth. By moving towards asset-backed currencies, these reforms aimed to eliminate the volatility and uncertainty that had plagued financial markets. In evaluating the long-term effects of these changes on global trade, investment patterns, and economic resilience, highlights how the reforms contributed to a more stable and predictable economic environment conducive to growth and innovation.

Environmental and Social Sustainability

Integral to NESARA and GESARA was the emphasis on sustainability, not just in economic terms but also regarding environmental stewardship and social welfare. This section explores how the acts facilitated investments in green technologies, supported sustainable development projects, and promoted policies that balanced economic growth with ecological preservation. Through narratives of communities transformed by these initiatives, it showcases the broader implications of the acts on promoting a sustainable and equitable future.

Challenges and Critiques

Despite their successes, NESARA and GESARA were not without their challenges and critics. This section addresses the hurdles encountered in implementing such comprehensive reforms, from bureaucratic inertia and political opposition to concerns about global autonomy and sovereignty. It also considers critiques regarding the pace of implementation, the adequacy of measures to prevent future financial crises, and the acts' effectiveness in addressing all dimensions of economic inequality.

The Legacy of Economic Reform

In reflecting on the legacy of NESARA and GESARA, this chapter posits that these acts were foundational in creating a more equitable, stable, and sustainable global economic system. It contemplates the lasting impact of the reforms on future generations, considering how the principles embedded in these acts will continue to influence global economic policies and practices. By evaluating both the achievements and the shortcomings of NESARA and GESARA, this section provides a balanced perspective on their role in transforming the global economic landscape.

This segment delves into the transformative potential of NESARA and GESARA, assessing their crucial influence on global economics, environmental sustainability, and societal well-being. Through comprehensive exploration of their effects, challenges, and persistent contributions, the chapter enhances our comprehension of the ways in which bold economic initiatives can trigger significant and enduring change worldwide.

Envisioning the Future Beyond 2060

As the narrative arc from 2025 to 2060 draws to a close, the world stands on the precipice of a future shaped by unprecedented change. The transformative impact of NESARA and GESARA, technological innovations, and a global commitment to peace and sustainability have collectively ushered in an era of prosperity and well-being previously unimaginable. Yet, the journey does not end here. We contemplate the legacy of the past 35 years and look forward to the challenges and opportunities that lie ahead, envisioning the future beyond 2060.

The Legacy of Transformation

The era from 2025 to 2060 will be remembered as a time when humanity collectively navigated the complexities of global challenges, leveraging innovative solutions and collaborative efforts to create a more equitable and sustainable world. This section reflects on the key lessons learned during this transformative period, emphasizing the importance of visionary leadership, technological advancement, and international cooperation in driving systemic change. It considers how the principles embedded in NESARA and GESARA, the advancements in healthcare, energy, and agriculture, and the strides towards global peace have laid a robust foundation for future generations.

Future Challenges

Despite the remarkable progress achieved, the future holds its own set of challenges. As the global population continues to grow and technological advancements accelerate, issues such as resource management, digital ethics, and interstellar exploration will demand attention. Exploring potential future challenges is essential, utilizing insights from experts and futurists. The discussion highlights the need for adaptable governance models, persistent innovation in sustainability, and robust ethical frameworks to successfully navigate the complexities of our increasingly interconnected and technologically sophisticated world.

Opportunities for Advancement

With challenges come opportunities for further advancement. This section delves into the potential for ongoing technological innovation to address future needs, from quantum computing and artificial intelligence to advancements in biotechnology and space exploration. It highlights the opportunities for enhancing global well-being, advancing human knowledge, and expanding our presence beyond Earth. Exploring emerging technologies and scientific boundaries inspires optimism for humanity's ability to tackle complex challenges and reach new accomplishments.

Envisioning the World of Tomorrow

Finally, we invite readers to envision the world of tomorrow, a world that continues to build on the achievements of the 2025-2060 era. It paints a picture of a future where sustainability, equity, and innovation are at the heart of human endeavor. Through speculative scenarios and imaginative explorations, this section encourages readers to consider how the decisions and actions of today will shape the legacy of tomorrow. It emphasizes the role of each individual in contributing to a future that honors the lessons of the past while embracing the possibilities of the future.

We close the narrative on a note of hopeful anticipation, recognizing the incredible journey of transformation that has occurred while acknowledging the work that remains. It stands as a testament to human ingenuity and resilience, offering a vision of the future that is both challenging and inspiring. As the world moves beyond 2060, the legacy of this era of unprecedented change will continue to influence the course of human history, guiding us toward a future filled with promise and potential.

Conclusion

Summarizing the Journey to Utopia

The journey from 2024 to 2060 is a testament to human resilience, ingenuity, and the enduring quest for a better world. This remarkable period, characterized by significant political leadership, technological advancements, and economic reforms, marked the transition towards what many would describe as a utopian society. Reflecting on this transformative era, it becomes evident how the confluence of visionary ideas and pragmatic actions reshaped the global landscape.

The Catalyst of Change: Political Leadership

At the heart of this transformation was the bold and sometimes contentious leadership of Donald Trump, whose presidency acted as a catalyst for change. His unconventional approach to diplomacy and economic policy not only resolved long-standing conflicts but also inspired a global movement towards economic reform and international cooperation. The successful implementation of NESARA in the United States, followed by the global adoption of GESARA, set new standards for financial equity and stability, proving the power of visionary political leadership to effectuate profound global changes.

Technological Renaissance: Shaping the Future

Parallel to the political shifts were the technological advancements that fundamentally altered human existence. Breakthroughs in Medbed technology, renewable energy, and sustainable agriculture addressed some of the most pressing challenges of the time, including healthcare, environmental degradation, and food security. These innovations not only improved the quality of life but also ensured the sustainability of the planet for future generations. The role of technology in this era cannot be overstated—it was both a driver of change and a facilitator of the utopian vision.

Economic Reforms: Laying the Foundation for Equity

The economic reforms brought about by NESARA and GESARA were pivotal in creating a more equitable and prosperous world. By eliminating debt, restructuring the global banking system, and introducing asset-backed currencies, these reforms addressed the root causes of economic disparity. The global economy witnessed unparalleled stability and growth, lifting millions out of poverty and fostering a sense of shared prosperity. The success of these economic reforms underscored the importance of re-imagining financial systems to serve the needs of all people.

A Tapestry of Change

The journey from 2024 to 2060 is a rich tapestry woven from the threads of political audacity, technological innovation, and economic transformation. It tells the story of a world that dared to envision a better future and then set about creating it. This era saw the dismantling of old paradigms and the birth of new ones, driven by the collective will to achieve a utopian vision.

As we reflect on this transformative period, it becomes clear that the journey to utopia was not just about the destinations reached but also about the lessons learned along the way. It was a testament to the power of human creativity, the resilience of the human spirit, and the unyielding belief in the possibility of a better world. This chapter not only summarizes the monumental shifts that occurred but also celebrates the indomitable will to aspire, achieve, and advance toward a utopian ideal.

Lessons for a Sustainable Future

As we stand at the threshold of the future, reflecting on the transformative journey from 2024 to 2060 offers invaluable insights into the essence of creating and sustaining a utopian society. The strides made in political leadership, technological innovation, and economic reform have not only reshaped our world but also imparted critical lessons on unity, innovation, and vision—lessons that will guide humanity as it navigates the complexities of the future.

The Power of Unity and International Cooperation

One of the most enduring lessons of this era is the paramount importance of unity and international cooperation. The global challenges faced—from climate change to economic disparity—demanded a collective response, underscoring that no nation could thrive in isolation. The successes achieved in establishing global peace, environmental sustainability, and economic stability highlighted the strength found in collaboration. Future generations must carry forward this spirit of unity, recognizing that the most daunting challenges can be overcome when the world comes together with a shared purpose.

The Role of Innovation in Shaping the Future

Innovation has been the engine driving the remarkable progress of the past 36 years. Technological advancements have not only solved critical problems but also opened new frontiers for exploration and growth. The development of Medbed technology, renewable energy sources, and sustainable food production systems exemplifies how innovation, guided by ethical considerations and the common good, can lead to a better world for all. As humanity looks beyond

2060, fostering a culture of innovation—where creative thinking and technological exploration are encouraged and supported—will be crucial in addressing future challenges and unlocking new possibilities.

Maintaining a Vision for a Better World

Perhaps the most crucial lesson from this transformative period is the importance of maintaining a clear and compelling vision for the future. The changes that led to the utopian society of 2060 were driven by visionary leaders and citizens who dared to imagine a better world and then worked tirelessly to realize that vision. The progress made serves as a powerful reminder that envisioning a more equitable, sustainable, and peaceful world is the first step toward creating it. Future leaders and individuals must continue to dream boldly and act with conviction, guided by a vision that transcends immediate challenges and looks to the long-term well-being of humanity and the planet.

Charting the Course Forward

As we contemplate the future beyond 2060, the lessons of unity, innovation, and vision offer a blueprint for sustaining the utopian world that has been achieved and for facing the unknown challenges ahead. The journey of the past 36 years teaches us that with collective will, creative ingenuity, and forward-looking leadership, humanity can not only navigate the uncertainties of the future but also shape it in the image of our highest aspirations.

The reflections and lessons of this transformative era underscore the capacity of humanity to create profound and lasting change. As we move forward, let these lessons inspire continued efforts to build on the achievements of the past, ensuring that the legacy of this golden era endures. Guided by the principles of unity, innovation, and vision, humanity can continue to strive for a world that not only sustains but also enriches the lives of all its inhabitants, creating a lasting utopia for generations to come.

NESARA and GESARA Unveiled

NESARA (National Economic Security and Recovery Act) and GESARA (Global Economic Security and Recovery Act) are acronyms that have gained attention in various circles, often associated with theories of global economic reform and prosperity programs. While these concepts have garnered interest and speculation, it's crucial to understand their origins, purported objectives, and the debates surrounding their legitimacy.

Origins and Background:

NESARA is said to have originated as a set of proposed economic reforms in the United States during the late 20th century. According to proponents, the act aimed to address issues such as income inequality, banking system reforms, and the elimination of perceived corrupt practices within the financial and political systems.

GESARA, on the other hand, is an extension of NESARA, purportedly expanding its scope to encompass global economic restructuring and cooperation among nations.

Key Components and Objectives:

While specifics may vary depending on interpretations, proponents of NESARA and GESARA generally claim that these acts include provisions such as:

1. Debt Forgiveness: Alleged provisions for the forgiveness of certain types of debt, including credit card debt, mortgages, and student loans, aiming to alleviate financial burdens on individuals and stimulate economic growth.

2. Financial Reforms: Proposed restructuring of financial systems, including changes to banking regulations, the introduction of asset-backed currency, and the abolition of fractional reserve banking.

3. Prosperity Programs: Advocated implementation of programs to distribute wealth and resources more equitably among citizens, with the goal of fostering greater economic stability and well-being for all.

4. Transparency and Accountability: Alleged measures to increase transparency and accountability in government and financial institutions, aiming to combat corruption and restore public trust.

Debates and Controversies:

Despite the enthusiasm of some proponents, NESARA and GESARA remain highly controversial topics with skeptics raising several points of contention:

1. Lack of Official Confirmation: Critics argue that there is a lack of credible evidence to support the existence of NESARA and GESARA as actual legislative acts or global agreements. Skeptics often point to the absence of official announcements or endorsements from government authorities or international organizations.

2. Conspiracy Theories: The concepts of NESARA and GESARA have been intertwined with various conspiracy theories, leading some to dismiss them as fringe ideas lacking in substance or credibility.

3. Unrealistic Expectations: Critics contend that the ambitious goals outlined in NESARA and GESARA proposals, such as debt forgiveness on a massive scale and fundamental changes to global financial systems, are unrealistic and impractical to implement.

4. Potential for Exploitation: Skeptics caution against the potential for exploitation by individuals or groups seeking to profit from the promotion of NESARA and GESARA narratives, including scams and fraudulent schemes targeting vulnerable individuals.

Conclusion:

NESARA and GESARA represent intriguing concepts that have captured the imagination of many seeking solutions to economic challenges and inequalities. However, their legitimacy and feasibility remain subjects of debate and skepticism. While some view them as visionary proposals for transformative change, others regard them as speculative theories lacking in evidence and practicality. As discussions surrounding these concepts continue, it is essential to critically evaluate claims and remain vigilant against misinformation and exploitation.

The Revolution of Medbed Technology

The landscape of healthcare is undergoing a profound transformation, propelled by the revolutionary advancements in Medbed technology. At the forefront of this evolution lies a paradigm shift in how we perceive and approach healing, driven by the fusion of quantum principles, regenerative medicine, and cutting-edge engineering.

Scientific Principles:

Medbed technology operates at the nexus of quantum healing and regenerative medicine, leveraging the inherent intelligence of the body's cellular processes to diagnose and treat ailments at their root cause. By harnessing quantum principles such as entanglement and coherence, Medbeds facilitate healing on a molecular level, surpassing the limitations of conventional medical modalities.

Development and Implementation:

The journey of Medbed technology from concept to reality has been marked by collaboration and innovation. Scientists, engineers, and healthcare professionals have pooled their expertise to overcome technical challenges and refine the efficacy of Medbed treatments. Through iterative development and rigorous testing, Medbeds have transitioned from speculative concepts to tangible instruments of healing, deployed in healthcare facilities worldwide.

Transforming Healthcare:

The impact of Medbed technology on healthcare is nothing short of revolutionary. By eradicating diseases, restoring bodily functions, and even reversing the effects of aging, Medbed treatments have ushered in a new era of health and vitality. Personal testimonials and case studies serve as poignant reminders of the profound and life-changing benefits experienced by individuals and communities fortunate enough to access Medbed therapies.

Future Potential:

Looking ahead, the potential of Medbed technology knows no bounds. Ongoing research and development efforts are exploring new frontiers in personalized medicine, organ regeneration, and disease prevention. However, ethical considerations and regulatory challenges loom large, demanding careful deliberation to ensure the responsible and equitable deployment of this transformative technology.

The revolution of Medbed technology represents

not only a leap forward in healthcare but also a testament to the boundless ingenuity and compassion of the human spirit. As we navigate the complexities of this brave new world, let us remain steadfast in our commitment to harnessing technology for the betterment of humanity, ensuring that the benefits of Medbed treatments are accessible to all who stand to benefit.

NESARA, GESARA, and Medbed technology—are three pivotal elements that have significantly shaped the world from 2025 to 2060. Through detailed analysis and exploration, this comprehensive overview not only elucidates the mechanisms and impacts of these initiatives but also underscores their collective role in driving humanity toward a brighter, more equitable future.

Epilogue

As we cast our gaze towards the year 2060, we are greeted by a world transformed—a world characterized by peace, prosperity, and unparalleled advancements in technology and human well-being. Through the lens of individuals from diverse corners of the globe, we catch a glimpse of the remarkable progress and harmony that define life in this new era.

Reflections from Around the World:

In Tokyo, Japan, Keiko, a young scientist, marvels at the strides made in healthcare, where advanced medical technologies have eradicated once-debilitating diseases and extended human lifespan. With access to personalized medicine and genetic therapies, Keiko envisions a future where everyone enjoys vibrant health and vitality.

Meanwhile, in Nairobi, Kenya, Kofi, a farmer, reflects on the agricultural revolution that has transformed food production in Africa. Through sustainable farming practices and innovative technologies, Kofi and his community have achieved food security while preserving the rich biodiversity of their land.

In Rio de Janeiro, Brazil, Sofia, an environmental activist, celebrates the renaissance of nature and the restoration of ecosystems that were once on the brink of collapse. Through collective action and a renewed commitment to conservation, Sofia sees a world where humans live in harmony with the natural world, reaping the benefits of a healthy planet.

A Hopeful Outlook:

As we peer into this future landscape, we are filled with a sense of optimism and possibility. Despite the challenges we face, humanity's capacity for innovation and adaptation shines brightly, illuminating the path towards a thriving world for future generations.

In the face of adversity, we have demonstrated resilience and resolve, harnessing the power of science and collaboration to overcome obstacles and forge a brighter tomorrow. From renewable energy to sustainable agriculture, from advances in healthcare to strides in education and equality, we have embraced the opportunities of the 21st century with courage and ingenuity.

As we bid farewell to the pages of history and turn towards the horizon of the future, let us carry forward the lessons of the past and the dreams of today. Let us continue to innovate, to explore, and to strive for a world where peace, prosperity, and health are not just aspirations but realities for all. In the hands of humanity lies the power to shape our destiny—to create a world where every individual, regardless of race, creed, or circumstance, can flourish and thrive.

The journey ahead may be challenging, but with vision, determination, and a steadfast commitment to our shared humanity, we can build a future that surpasses even our wildest dreams. As the sun sets on one era and rises on another, let us step boldly into the unknown, confident in our ability to craft a world worthy of generations yet to come.

Bruce Goldwell's

Web Site

Www.MyKindleBooks.net

QFS, Nesara/Gesara, and 2060

https://amzn.to/496lzGs

Nesara/Gesara, and 2060" series, where you'll discover the keys to navigating the dynamic landscape of finance in the digital age. Dive into the world of cryptocurrencies, decentralized finance (DeFi), and blockchain technology as you uncover the potential of these groundbreaking innovations to revolutionize the way we interact with money, invest in assets, and conduct transactions.

In this comprehensive series, you'll explore the intricacies of cryptocurrencies such as Bitcoin, Ethereum, and Ripple (XRP), learning about their underlying technology, market dynamics, and investment opportunities. Gain insights into the principles of decentralized finance and explore the diverse ecosystem of DeFi platforms, protocols, and applications reshaping traditional financial services.

But the journey doesn't stop there. The "Cryptocurrency Unlocked" series also delves into broader topics shaping the future of finance, including the NESARA (National Economic Security and Recovery Act) and GESARA (Global Economic Security and Reformation

Act) initiatives, which propose radical reforms to the global financial system. Discover the potential implications of these ambitious plans and how they could reshape the economic landscape in the years to come.

Furthermore, the series explores the cutting-edge Quantum Financial System (QFS), a revolutionary paradigm that leverages quantum computing and blockchain technology to create a more secure, transparent, and efficient financial infrastructure. Learn about the principles behind the QFS and its potential to transform the way we transact, invest, and store value in the digital era.

Finally, journey into the future with the book "2060," a speculative exploration of the potential consequences of emerging technologies, societal trends, and geopolitical shifts on the world of finance. From AI-powered trading algorithms to digital currencies issued by central banks, "2060" offers a glimpse into a future where finance is more interconnected, automated, and decentralized than ever before.

Join us as we unlock the secrets of the new world of finance in the "QFS, Nesara/Gesara, and 2060" series. Whether you're a seasoned investor, a curious newcomer, or simply intrigued by the possibilities of the digital revolution, this series will empower you to navigate the complex landscape of finance in the 21st century and beyond.

About The Author

Bruce Goldwell, a beacon of inspiration, has journeyed from the depths of adversity to become a self-help/motivational author and the creative mind behind two spellbinding fantasy adventures: "Dragon Keepers," a captivating six-book series, and "Starfighters Defending Earth," an enthralling three-book series. But his story is not just about crafting tales; it's a testament to resilience and the transformative power of hope.

As a Vietnam veteran who endured over a decade of homelessness, Bruce faced profound challenges. Yet, in the crucible of adversity, he developed a compassionate heart and an unwavering desire to uplift others. During his years on the streets, Bruce sought solace and inspiration within the pages of motivational literature at local bookstores, finding resonance in the works of acclaimed authors like the creators of Chicken Soup for the Soul, Bob Proctor, and David Stanley, Elvis Presley's brother.

Inspired by the life-altering impact of "The Secret," Bruce Goldwell penned his first book, "Mastery of Abundant Living: The Keys to Mastering the Law of Attraction." His dedication to uplifting others reached new heights when he presented the first autographed copy to none other than Bob Proctor himself.

Understanding that traditional self-help material might not resonate with younger audiences, Bruce astutely crafted fantastical adventure series for teens. Through these enchanting stories, he seamlessly weaves principles of success and powerful life lessons, igniting hope and encouraging personal growth in the hearts of young readers.

Bruce Goldwell's journey from a homeless veteran to a prolific and impactful author isn't just a personal triumph—it's a global phenomenon. His books have resonated with thousands worldwide, sparking transformative journeys and empowering individuals to rewrite their own stories. Bruce's unwavering belief in the life-changing potential of his works showcases the boundless resilience, determination, and transformative power embedded in the written word. Support his impactful mission and join the countless others who have found inspiration in the stories and wisdom woven by Bruce Goldwell.

<u>Www.mykindlebooks.net</u>

Made in the USA
Columbia, SC
27 February 2025